On March 5, 1836, in the plaza of a crumbling Spanish mission called the Alamo, Colonel William B. Travis addressed his ragtag company of 184 men. Outside the walls of the old mission camped a Mexican army of several thousand soldiers under the command of General Antonio Lopez de Santa Anna. Santa Anna's army was preparing to take the Alamo by force.

Colonel William B. Travis

"Our fate is sealed," Travis told his men. For almost two weeks, the Alamo's defenders had held the mission. They had watched Santa Anna's army position itself for attack. And they had waited for help. But Travis's pleas for help from other forces fighting for Texas's independence had gone unanswered. So Travis had gathered the Alamo's defenders to tell them that no reinforcements were on the way.

The men with Travis had come to Texas from all over the United States and even from Europe. There were also nine *Tejanos*—native-born Mexicans fighting with the Texas army in support of independence from Mexico. Some of the defenders had lived in Texas for years. Others had just arrived. They had come looking for land, or for a fresh start in life, or simply for adventure. Their struggle at the Alamo was part of a conflict that would end in independence for Texas.

Some of the defenders were already famous. Colonel David Crockett was a legendary frontiersman who had served three terms in the United States Congress. When he left Congress, he gathered up a dozen or so other Tennesseans and headed for Texas. They had arrived at the Alamo only one month earlier.

Colonel Jim Bowie was known as an adventurer and dangerous duelist. His weapon of choice was a foot-long knife with a curved blade and a handle guard. It was called the Bowie knife. Bowie had been one of the first defenders to arrive at the Alamo, and he shared the command with Travis. But he had become seriously ill and was confined to his cot throughout the siege of the Alamo.

Colonel Jim Bowie

As they gathered on March 5, Travis explained to Crockett, Bowie, and the others how hopeless their situation was. Then he drew his sword. He walked from one end of the compound to the other, tracing a line in the sand with his sword. Travis told the men that anyone who wished to leave the Alamo was free to go. But those who would stay and fight should cross the line and stand with him.

Almost all of the defenders of the Alamo crossed the line and stood with Travis. Bowie even asked to be carried across the line on his cot. Only one man chose not to stay and fight.

None of the men who crossed Travis's line would survive. But by choosing to stay and fight, they entered history.

David Crockett was already famous as a frontiersman and United States congressman when he arrived at the Alamo.

According to legend, Colonel Travis drew a line in the sand with his sword when he appealed to his men to remain with him and defend the Alamo.

The first Europeans who came to the region that is now known as Texas were Spanish explorers who arrived in the early 1500s. They claimed the area as part of Spain's enormous empire in North America. At that time, Spain's territory extended from present-day Mexico to Oregon. During the next several centuries, the Spanish built missions and forts in what was then called New Spain. One of these was the mission named San Antonio de Valero, which was founded between 1716 and 1718 by Franciscan friars.

Missions were built by the Spanish to house the friars who attempted to bring Christianity to the American Indians.

The purpose of the mission of San Antonio de Valero was to bring Christianity to American

6

Indians who lived in the region. But the Friars' efforts were not successful. San Antonio de Valero was only in operation for a short time before it was abandoncd in 1793. The mission came into use again in the first decades of the 1800s. It was occupied by Spanish troops who used the mission as a barracks. It was during this time that the mission became known as the Alamo. The name came from the Spanish word for the cottonwood trees that grew in the area.

Missions like the Alamo helped the Spanish maintain their claim to the land in North America. But the Spanish claim to Texas did not stop others from exploring the area, or even from trying to take control of it away from Spain. The French explorer René-Robert Sieur de La Salle had traveled up and down the Mississippi River in the late 1600s. When Great Britain's American colonies gained independence in 1783, Spain feared that the new nation would begin to grow westward and set its sights on Texas.

Indeed, in 1801, an American named Philip Nolan led a force of armed men into Texas, where they encountered Spanish soldiers. In the fighting that followed, Nolan was killed and nine of his men were captured. But this incident did not discourage other American filibusters—military adventurers—from going into the region.

La Salle

Thomas Jefferson

Part of the land included in the Louisiana Purchase had already been claimed by Spain.

Even the United States government itself laid a claim to Texas. In 1803, the United States bought an enormous tract of land just west of the Mississippi River from France. It was called the Louisiana Purchase. No boundary was marked between Texas and the purchased land just to the north. President Thomas Jefferson, therefore, claimed Texas as part of the purchase. Spain disputed Jefferson's claim. Armies from both countries rushed into the region. No shots were fired, but the boundary remained in dispute.

By this time, however, the Spanish empire in North America was weakening. It faced numerous challenges inside and outside its

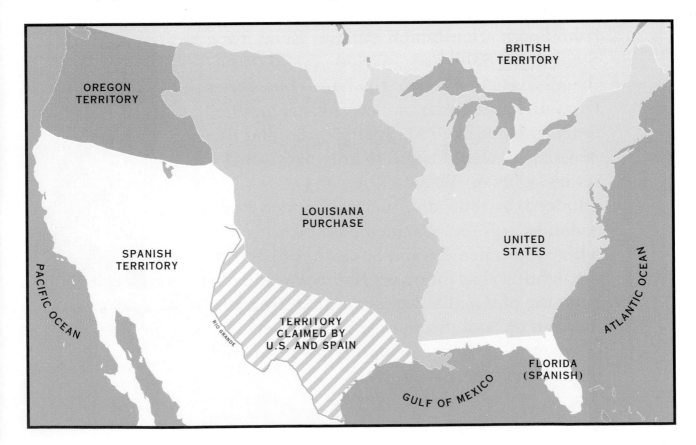

borders. Spain managed to defeat a Mexican rebellion in 1810 and another uprising in Texas in 1813. And in 1819, a filibuster from Mississippi named Dr. James Long managed to take two Texas towns from Spanish control before he was finally captured.

Mexico won its independence from Spain in 1821, after a bloody, decade-long struggle. With independence, Mexico also gained control over Texas. But Mexico had as much difficulty as Spain did controlling the vast and mostly unsettled territory.

After three centuries of Spanish control, only a tiny portion of Texas was populated. In fact, only three towns emerged from the Spanish colonial era: San Antonio de Béxar (later called San Antonio), La Bahia del Espiritu Santo (Goliad), and Nacogdoches. But settlers were on their way. In the easternmost part of Texas, American settlers led by Stephen F. Austin contracted first with Spain, then with Mexico, to settle a colony in Texas. For a small investment, each male head of a family was given 640 acres (259 hectares) of land, with additional land for women and children. Austin served as the governor of the colony. Elsewhere, other settlers from the United States took a less lawful approach. They simply squatted, or settled, on public land that they did not legally own.

Stephen F. Austin

Stephen F. Austin (black coat) and a Mexican land commissioner (center) distribute land to American settlers.

In 1824, the newly independent Mexican government drafted a constitution that made Texas part of the state of Coahuila y Texas. States were given the power to run their own affairs, so Coahuila y Texas threw open its doors to more immigrants. Americans looking for a fresh start looked toward Texas. They saw millions of acres of good land available at affordable prices. The only requirement was that the settlers become Mexican citizens. It appeared to be such a good deal that hundreds of Americans poured into Texas. By 1834, about nine thousand people lived in Texas. But trouble was brewing.

With more families moving into Texas from the United States, differences between the

Americans and their Mexican governors often turned into conflicts. The Americans spoke a different language, came from a different culture, and many belonged to different religions from the Mexicans. Simple misunderstandings sometimes blossomed into armed conflicts.

The tension became worse in 1833, when General Santa Anna was installed as president of Mexico. Before long, he was ruling as a dictator. He restricted immigration by Anglo-Americans, stopped the importation of slaves, and announced military occupation of Texas. All these changes angered the American settlers.

General Antonio Lopez de Santa Anna

Stephen Austin traveled to Mexico City to negotiate with Santa Anna.

When Stephen F. Austin traveled to Mexico City to ask Santa Anna to reconsider some of his policies, Austin was imprisoned. By the time he made his way back to Texas two years later, Austin was convinced that only war would resolve the differences between the settlers and Santa Anna. In a letter to his cousin, Austin wrote, "A great immigration from Kentucky, Tennessee, etc., each man with his rifle or musket, would be of great use to us—very great indeed."

Increasingly, Americans living in Texas began to think that the future of Texas lay not with Mexico, but with the United States. Much of Texas's soil was ideal for growing cotton, the main crop of the slave-holding American South. Texans reasoned that they would be welcome in the United States as a slave state. "We must and ought to become a part of the United States. . . Texas must be slave country," Austin declared. Recent immigrants to Texas, most of whom had come from slave-holding states, agreed. But Santa Anna was determined to maintain Mexico's hold on Texas.

Posters appealed to Texans to defend their homes and families against Santa Anna.

FRIENDS

AND

CITIZENS OF TEXAS

Information, of a character not to be questioned, has just been received from Col. Fannin, which states that Santa Ana, at the head of four thousand men, has crossed the San Antonio river, leaving Goliad in his rear, and is moving upon our public stores, and thence to Gonsales. This force is independent of the army under Siexma before Bejar A general turn out has commenced and is going on here and westward, and as far as known. Citisens in every part of the country, it is hoped, will be no less ready to defend their homes, their wives, and children.

We advise that every armed vessel which can be had should be despatched at once, to scour the Gulf, and all points where most likely to interespt the stores and supplies of the enamy, and every precaution adopted for protecting our own stores.

JOHN R. JONES, } *Standing*
THOMAS GAY, } *Committee.*

San Felipe, March 2, 1836.

In the summer of 1835, disputes between the Mexican government and American settlers in Texas flared. Word came that Santa Anna was replacing the state government of Coahuila y Texas with military rule and that Santa Anna himself was leading an army there to take control. The Texans reacted quickly. Colonel William B. Travis, who had come to Texas in 1831, rounded up twenty-five men and drove a Mexican garrison out of the town of Anahuac.

In September, the Mexican colonel in command at San Antonio ordered the small town of Gonzales, located about 50 miles (80 kilometers) east of San Antonio, to give up a small cannon that the town used for defense. Instead of giving it up, the townspeople buried it in a peach orchard. The small force of Mexican soldiers who were sent for the cannon were taken prisoner. As a result, Texas prepared itself for war. "Every man in Texas is called upon to take up arms in defense of his country and his rights," read one announcement.

The chance to fight was on its way. Angered by the town's disobedience, a force of one hundred Mexican cavalry approached Gonzales. The cavalry was met by a force of 160 Texas volunteers. The Texans marched

The townspeople of Gonzales refused to turn the town's cannon over to the Mexicans.

under a flag that depicted a cannon with the motto "Come and Take It." The rebels charged the Mexican troops and chased them back to San Antonio, suffering no casualties. This was the beginning of the fight for Texas's independence.

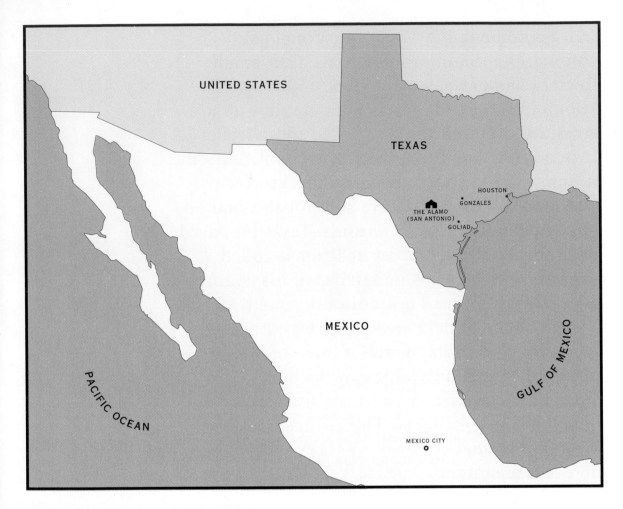

UNITED STATES

TEXAS

HOUSTON
GONZALES
THE ALAMO
(SAN ANTONIO)
GOLIAD

MEXICO

PACIFIC OCEAN

GULF OF MEXICO

MEXICO CITY

The Alamo became a symbol of the struggle for control between Mexico and Texas.

One week later, the Texans captured an undermanned Mexican fortress at Goliad, 85 miles (137 km) southeast of San Antonio. The victory supplied the rebels with hundreds of muskets, rifles, bayonets, and cannonballs.

In November, a group of the rebellion's leaders met in San Felipe, Texas, to discuss whether Texas should declare its independence from Mexico. While all agreed that independence would eventually occur, they decided against writing an actual Declaration of Independence. Instead, the leaders agreed to publish a Declaration of Causes that would guarantee their right to live on Mexican soil. They also named General Sam Houston, a veteran soldier and associate of United States president Andrew Jackson, the commander-in-chief of the army.

Meanwhile, the volunteer army that had won at Gonzales and Goliad was now laying siege to the Mexican troops in San Antonio. On December 5, 1835, the Texans roared into the town, driving the Mexicans back street by street. After three days of fierce fighting, the Mexican soldiers withdrew into the Alamo, the old Spanish mission. They held out there— the rebels peppering the walls of the mission with cannon fire—for two more days before surrendering. The Mexican troops were allowed to return to Mexico after promising they would not return to Texas armed.

Sam Houston was appointed to be the commander-in-chief of the Texas forces.

With winter approaching, many of the Texas volunteers headed home. They had defeated Mexican troops in several battles, taken control of three towns from the Mexicans, and suffered few casualties in the process. But they also knew that the greatest test was still ahead. General Santa Anna was said to be gathering a huge army for the march north to Texas. The Mexican president was determined to defeat the Texans and return control of Texas to Mexico.

General Houston knew that preparations had to be made to defend Texas against Santa

General Santa Anna assembled an army of five thousand soldiers for the march to Texas.

Anna's army. But with many of his volunteers gone, he had few choices. "I was a general without an army," he wrote later. On January 17, 1836, he sent his friend, Jim Bowie, and twenty-five men to San Antonio. Fewer than one hundred Texans had remained in the town since it was taken from the Mexicans. Houston had instructed Bowie to examine the Alamo and decide if it could be defended.

The townspeople of San Antonio were fond of Bowie and convinced him and his men to stay and defend the Alamo. They offered him supplies and assistance. Soon after, Bowie wrote in a letter that he had "come to the solemn resolution that we will rather die in these ditches than give it (the Alamo) up to the enemy."

William Travis arrived at the Alamo on February 2, 1836, with thirty troops. He and Bowie agreed to share the command of the troops gathered at the Alamo. By then, there were about 140 men holding the mission.

The first action the two commanders agreed upon was a call for help. They wrote to the governor of Texas requesting supplies, munitions, men, and money. It was the first of many pleas for assistance the defenders would make. Like most of the other pleas, it went unanswered. Meanwhile, Bowie took ill. His condition worsened until he was unable to rise from his cot. Travis then took over full command.

FREEMEN OF TEXAS
To Arms!!! To Arms!!!!
"Now 's the day, & now's the hour."

CAMP OF THE VOLUNTEERS,
Friday Night, 11 o'clock;
October 2, 1835.

Fellow Citizens:—
We have prevailed on our fellow citizen Wm. H. Wharton, Esq. to return and communicate to you the following express, and also to urge as many as can by possibility leave their homes to repair to Gonzales immediately, "armed and equipped for war even to the knife." On the receipt of this intelligence the Volunteers immediately resolved to march to Gonzales to aid their countrymen. We are just now starting which must apologize for the brevity of this communication. We refer you to Mr. Wharton for an explanation of our wishes, opinions and intentions, and also for

such political information as has come into our hands. If Texas will now act promptly; she will soon be redeemed from that worse than Egyptian bondage which now cramps her resources and retards her prosperity.

DAVID RANDON,
WM. J. BRYAND,
J. W. FANNIN, Jr.
F. T. WELLS,
GEO. SUTHERLAND'
B. T. ARCHER,
W. D. C. HALL,
W. H. JACK,
WM. T. AUSTIN,
P. D. McNEEL.

P. S. An action took place on yesterdy at Gonzales, in which the Mexican Commander and several soldiers were slain—no loss on the American side

Help did come, however, from David Crockett and his group of fourteen volunteers from Tennessee. The group arrived at the Alamo on February 9, 1836. Travis offered the legendary Crockett a position of authority. But the fifty-year-old former congressman declined. "Assign me some place," he told Travis, "and I and my Tennessee boys will defend it all right." Crockett's arrival boosted the morale of the troops at the Alamo. They celebrated at a dance given in Crockett's honor. But they did not have much time to celebrate. Santa Anna and his army were approaching. On February 23, they arrived.

Santa Anna brought five thousand men and a long supply train that came rumbling into San Antonio. He had spent the equivalent of $7.5 million preparing and outfitting his army. The forces at the Alamo were not so grandly supplied. "If there has ever been a dollar here," one defender had written, "I have no knowledge of it."

Santa Anna's arrival took Travis by surprise. The Alamo defenders knew the Mexican general eventually would attack. But they thought he would wait until later in the spring, when there would be more grass on the prairie for his horses and livestock to graze. But one day, a scouting party from the Alamo rode almost directly into the advancing Mexican army. The scouting party barely escaped to ride back to the Alamo and warn the defenders.

Santa Anna's army was better equipped and better trained than the defenders at the Alamo.

Travis hurriedly gathered his men, supplies, and a few refugees from town into the Alamo compound. Already low on supplies, his men rounded up thirty head of cattle and found eighty or ninety bushels of corn.

Travis sent another message to the mayor of Gonzales, asking for reinforcements. Then he sent a different kind of message to the gathering Mexican army. He had the Alamo's largest cannon fire off a defiant shot. The Mexicans answered with several blasts of their own, which landed in the compound but did no damage. They also raised a red-colored flag over the town. Word was sent to the defenders that Santa Anna would show no mercy. He ordered the death of every defender at the Alamo.

On the night of February 24, 1836, Travis wrote one of the most famous letters in American history. When the letter finally made its way to the small towns of Texas and to the United States, it helped ensure that the Alamo would be remembered throughout the fight for Texas independence and beyond. But the letter was far too late to help the doomed defenders of the Alamo.

The letter was addressed "To the People of Texas and All Americans in the World." Travis wrote that he and his men were under siege and had been ordered by Santa Anna to surrender. "I have answered the demand with a cannon shot and our flag still waves proudly from the walls," he wrote. "I shall never surrender or retreat. I call on you in the name of Liberty, of patriotism [and] everything dear to the American character, to come to our aid. . . . If this call is neglected, I

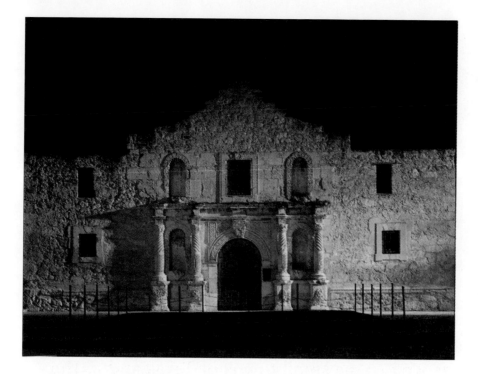

The night before the fighting began, Colonel Travis wrote a now-famous letter to "All Americans in the World," in which he vowed that he would rather die than surrender the Alamo to the Mexicans.

am determined . . . to die like a soldier who never forgets what is due to his own honor [and] that of his country—Victory or Death!"

The defenders of the Alamo could look over the walls of the mission and see the Mexican troops moving into position to attack. The Mexicans were dressed in dazzling uniforms. They paraded in formation. Thousands of them camped on every side of the Alamo. The defenders themselves wore only everyday, non-military clothes in which to fight. They carried an array of weapons—muskets, long rifles, and hunting knives. They busied themselves preparing the mission for the attack that was sure to come.

Inside the Alamo, the defenders prepared for Santa Anna's attack.

They didn't have to wait long. On February 25, 1836, the morning after Travis wrote his historic letter, the Mexicans attacked. Between two hundred and three hundred troops advanced on the south wall of the mission. The defenders held their fire. When the attackers were at point-blank range, the cannons on the Alamo walls opened fire. The frontier marksmen took lethal aim with their long rifles. Before long, the Mexican column fell back to take cover behind some small huts outside the Alamo.

Two defenders rode out from the south gate of the Alamo with torches. Under heavy gunfire from the Mexicans, they set fire to many of the huts. Deprived of their cover, the Mexicans fell back again. The Texans had survived their first test, suffering no casualties. But they knew that this attack was only the beginning.

During the next several days, more Mexican troops and artillery took up positions around the Alamo. The circle of Mexicans tightened around the fortress. Still, the troops inside the Alamo were able to get messages through the Mexican lines. On March 1, they even received some help from outside. A group of thirty-two volunteers had ridden from Gonzales, past the Mexican army, and into the Alamo. They had come in response to Travis's plea for reinforcements. They increased the number of defenders to 184. Still, they were facing a Mexican force of several thousand.

Santa Anna's troops surrounded the Alamo on all sides.

Travis needed more help—not just troops, but supplies, guns, and ammunition. A force of two hundred Texans with artillery had left nearby Goliad to relieve the Alamo. But after only a few miles, their wagons broke down. Unable to move their supplies and canon, they turned back.

To keep up morale in the Alamo, David Crockett moved throughout the mission, encouraging the troops. In the evening, he entertained and distracted them with fiddle playing and storytelling. He even became a familiar character to the enemy. Don Rafael Santana, one of Santa Anna's captains, later remembered one of the Alamo defenders: "He wore a buckskin suit and a cap all of a pattern entirely different from the suits worn by his comrades. . . . We all learned to keep a good distance when he was seen to make ready to shoot. He rarely missed his mark. . . . This man I later learned was known as [Crockett]."

Miles from the Alamo, unknown to Crockett and the rest of the defenders, the movement toward independence from Mexico continued. On March 2, delegates to a Texas convention finally signed a Declaration of Independence. Word of the declaration would never reach the defenders of the Alamo.

The defenders knew only that the Mexican army was inching closer, tightening its grip on the Alamo. When the sun rose on March 5, 1836,

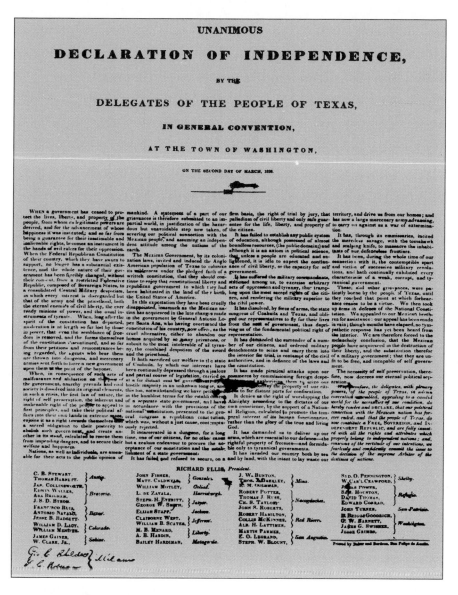

The Texas Declaration of Independence was signed on March 2, 1836. The defenders at the Alamo never knew that independence from Mexico had finally been achieved.

the defenders could see that Mexican cannons had been moved to within 200 yards (183 meters) of the Alamo. All that day, the Mexican cannons bombarded the mission. The Texans were running low on ammunition. They could do little more than take cover and wait for nightfall.

That night, Travis assembled his troops, and drew his line in the sand. The men who crossed the line to stand with Travis understood that they were accepting almost certain death. But the defenders believed in their fight for independence, and were willing to give their lives to achieve it. Sure enough, the next morning they were awakened by Mexican bugle calls. The final assault was about to begin.

The Mexican infantry, artillery, and cavalry had formed battle lines. On a signal, the Mexican troops rushed toward the walls of the mission. The Texans unleashed a fearsome artillery barage that repelled the first two charges. Finally, the third charge reached the Alamo's walls. Travis and many of the defenders

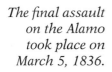
The final assault on the Alamo took place on March 5, 1836.

ran to defend the north wall, the Alamo's weakest point of defense. The Alamo's cannons leveled wave after wave of attackers. But the defenders could not load and reload quickly enough. Soon they were overrun by attacking troops.

Travis was one of the first defenders to be killed. With the enemy pouring into the compound, the Texans fell back into the Alamo's central plaza. There they fired at the attacking troops, taking a heavy toll. But more breaches were opened in the Alamo's walls. Mexican troops poured in. Amid the noise and confusion, one of the Texans grabbed a torch and headed for the room where the defenders' gunpowder was stored. He planned to blow up the Alamo rather than have it taken by the Mexicans. But he was killed before he could reach the gunpowder.

The 184 defenders of the Alamo were no match for the 5,000 Mexican soldiers.

Susanna Dickinson

The Mexican troops rushed from room to room in the Alamo compound, killing every defender they could find. Bowie was killed in his cot. In the mission chapel, the Mexicans came upon the few women, children, and slaves who had remained in the Alamo. The Mexicans marched them away from the battle scene. Susanna Dickinson, the wife of Travis's artillery commander and the only adult survivor of the seige, reported seeing Crockett's body outside the chapel.

The final battle lasted less than an hour. When the fighting died down, the sun was just beginning to rise. But the destruction was terrible. None of the Alamo's defenders survived. Approximately 1,500 Mexicans were killed. The Alamo once again belonged to Mexico. But it had come at an enormous price.

Santa Anna had spent a total of two weeks besieging the Alamo. During the next several weeks, Mexican armies would crush several more outmanned Texan forces. But then, six weeks after the Alamo, Santa Anna ran into General Sam Houston's army at the Battle of San Jacinto.

By that time, Houston's men had learned of the fate of their comrades at the Alamo. Shouting "Remember the Alamo," they defeated Santa Anna's army, captured the general himself, and won independence for Texas. Texas was an independent country, called the Republic of Texas, from 1836 to 1845. In 1845, Texas joined the United States as the twenty-eighth state in the Union.

Today, the Alamo stands as a reminder of the battle and its importance to the histories of both the United States and Mexico.

Each year, thousands of people from throughout the world visit the Alamo.

GLOSSARY

artillery – mounted guns, such as cannons

barracks – building used to house soldiers

breaches – breaks that provide openings in a wall or line of defense

casualties – soldiers who are missing in action, or have been killed or wounded in battle

duelist – person who takes part in a prearranged combat to settle a disagreement

Colonel Jim Bowie was an adventurer and duelist.

filibuster – military adventurer who is not part of a regular army

Franciscan – order of friars associated with St. Francis of Assisi

garrison – body of troops stationed in a fortified place

immigration – the movement of people to a new land

Louisiana Purchase – territory purchased from France by the United States, extending from the Rocky Mountains to the Mississippi River and from the Gulf of Mexico to Canada

munitions – materials used in war, such as weapons and ammunition

Louisiana Purchase

ragtag – hastily assembled group

reinforcements – additional troops

veteran – person who has done long service in an occupation or activity

TIMELINE

1716
1718 } Mission San Antonio de Valero established

American colonies gain independence **1783**

Mission San Antonio de Valero abandoned **1793**

1803 Louisiana Purchase

1810
} Mexican War for Independence
1821

1824 Mexican state of Coahuila y Texas formed

Santa Anna becomes president of Mexico **1833**
Texas War for Independence begins **1835**
1836

Texas becomes 28th state in the Union **1845**

Battle of the
Alamo; Republic
of Texas formed

INDEX *(Boldface page numbers indicate illustrations.)*

PHOTO CREDITS

©: Archive Photos: 7, 8, 11, 13, 26, 31 bottom right, 31 left; Archives Division, Texas State Library: 3; Corbis-Bettmann: 4 bottom, 5 top, 10, 15, 30 top; The Daughters of the Republic of Texas Libary at the Alamo: 5 bottom, 23, 28 bottom; Eric von Schmidt: 27; Friends of The Governor's Mansion, Austin, Texas: 28 top; H. Armstrong Roberts: 29 (R. Kord); North Wind Picture Archives: 6, 9, 16; Root Resources: 2 (Mary A. Root); Stock Montage, Inc.: 4 top, 12, 18, 19, 25; Superstock, Inc.: cover, 22; Tom Stack & Associates: 1, 31 top right (Brian Parker), 21 (Manfred Gottschalk).

Maps by TJS Design

ABOUT THE AUTHOR

Andrew Santella is a lifelong resident of Chicago. He is a graduate of Chicago's Loyola University, where he studied American literature. He writes about history, sports, and popular culture for several magazines for young people. He is the author of these other Children's Press titles: *The Capitol* and *Jackie Robinson Breaks the Color Line* (Cornerstones of Freedom) and *Mo Vaughn* (Sports Stars).

The Water Of Life

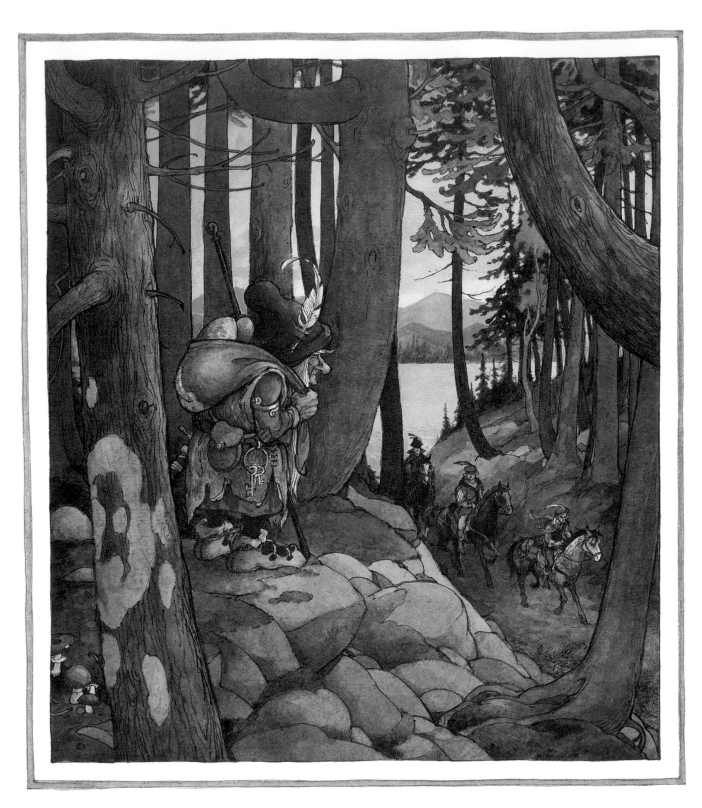

The Water Of Life

A TALE FROM THE BROTHERS GRIMM

· RETOLD BY ·

Barbara Rogasky

· ILLUSTRATED BY ·

Trina Schart Hyman

Holiday House

NEW YORK

1986 A.D.

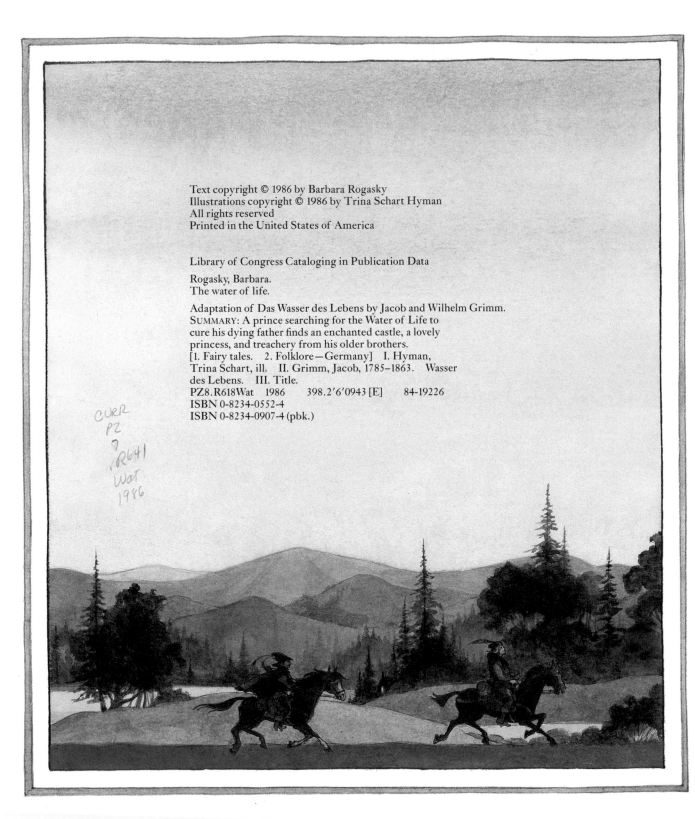

Library of Congress Cataloging in Publication Data

Rogasky, Barbara.
The water of life.

Adaptation of Das Wasser des Lebens by Jacob and Wilhelm Grimm.
SUMMARY: A prince searching for the Water of Life to
cure his dying father finds an enchanted castle, a lovely
princess, and treachery from his older brothers.
[1. Fairy tales.   2. Folklore—Germany]   I. Hyman,
Trina Schart, ill.   II. Grimm, Jacob, 1785–1863.   Wasser
des Lebens.   III. Title.
PZ8.R618Wat   1986   398.2'6'0943 [E]   84-19226
ISBN 0-8234-0552-4
ISBN 0-8234-0907-4 (pbk.)

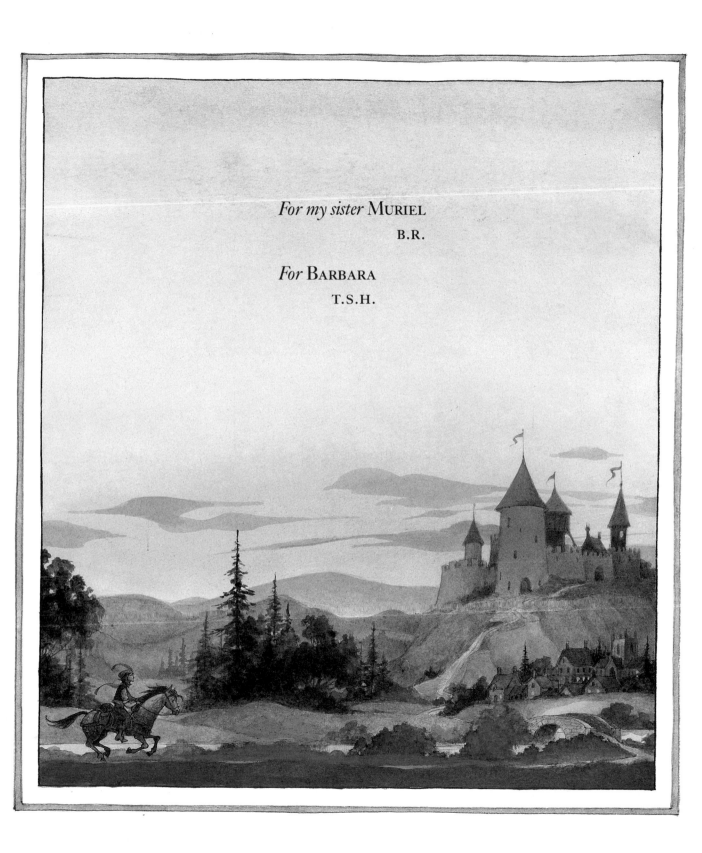

For my sister MURIEL

B.R.

For BARBARA

T.S.H.

Once upon a time there was a king who became so sick that everyone believed he would die. His three sons were very sad. One day they went to the castle gardens, where they wept in sorrow.

A little old man came over to them and asked, "Why are you crying?"

They explained that their father was dying of a terrible sickness, and that there was no cure.

"I know a cure," said the little old man. "It's the Water of Life. If he drinks it, the king will be well again. But it is very hard to find."

The oldest son said, "I'll find it." He went to his father to ask permission.

The king shook his head weakly. "No," he said. "The danger is too great. I would rather die."

The son begged and pleaded, telling his father how much he loved him. But secretly he thought, "If I find this Water of Life and my father is cured, he will leave his kingdom to me when he dies."

The king believed his son's love was pure, and finally he gave his permission.

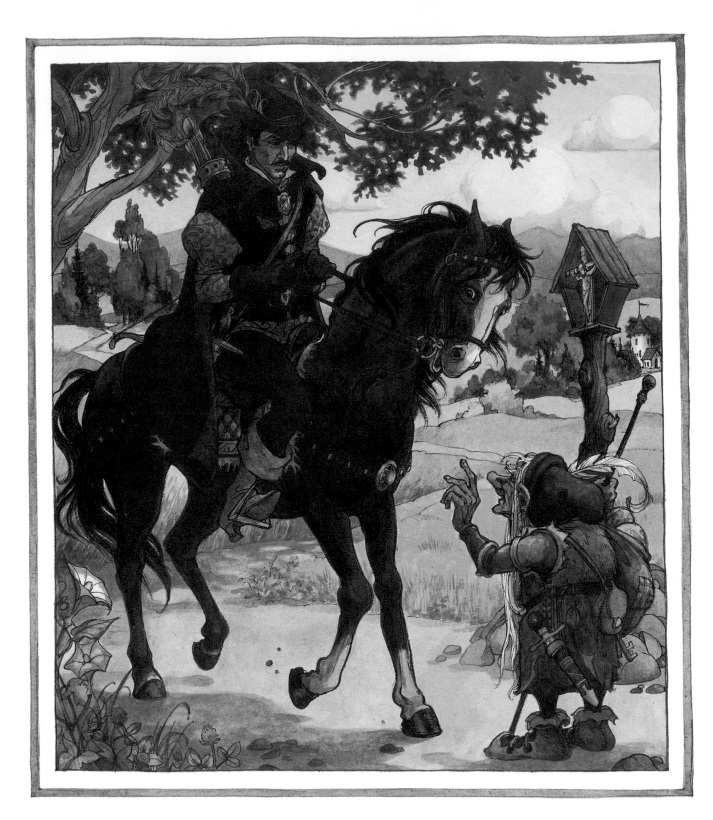

The prince set off on his journey. In a little while, he came upon a dwarf who stood in the middle of the road. "Where are you going so fast?" the dwarf asked.

The prince, who had to stop his horse, was greatly annoyed. "Stupid runt," he said. "That's no business of yours." And he rode proudly away, his nose in the air.

The little man was very angry, and he cursed the king's oldest son.

Soon the prince came to a steep-sided ravine between two mountains. As he rode along, the ravine became narrower and narrower, until it was barely wide enough for the prince and his horse to pass through. Finally it became so narrow that they got stuck. No matter how much he pushed or poked or prodded or yelled, the prince and his horse could move neither forward nor backward. So there they stayed, wedged between the walls of the ravine.

The king waited a long time for his oldest son to return, but he did not come back. And the king grew sicker and sicker.

One day his second son came to him and asked permission to look for the Water of Life.

Weaker than ever, the king shook his head. "No," he said. "The danger is too great. I would rather die."

"Please, Father," his second son said. "Let me go out of love for you." But to himself he was saying, as his brother had said, "If I find this Water of Life and my father is cured, the kingdom will be mine when he dies."

The king believed his second son's love was pure, and at last he gave his permission.

The prince set off. Before long, he too came upon the dwarf standing in the middle of the road. "Where are you going so fast?" the dwarf asked.

The prince had stopped his horse. "Idiot midget," he said. "That's none of your business." And he almost ran over the dwarf in his proud haste to get away.

The tiny man, angry again, cursed the king's second son.

The prince came to a steep-sided ravine, and the same thing happened. The farther he rode, the narrower it became, until finally he was stuck fast and could move neither forward nor backward. This is what happens to those who have too much pride.

When the second son did not return, the youngest went to his father and asked his leave to seek the Water of Life. So weak he could barely speak, the king gave his permission.

On his journey the prince came upon the dwarf, who asked him where he was hurrying so fast. He stopped the horse and explained. "I am searching for the Water of Life, because my father is so sick he is dying."

"Do you know how to find it?" the dwarf asked.

"No," said the prince.

"Since you have not been too proud to answer me, the way your brothers were," the dwarf said, "I'll tell you where the Water of Life is and help you get it. There is a fountain in the courtyard of an enchanted castle, and the Water of Life flows from that. But you will never get in unless you do exactly as I say."

The prince listened carefully.

The dwarf said, "Here is an iron rod and two loaves of bread. Knock on the castle gate three times with the rod, and it will open. In the courtyard there are two lions with huge gaping jaws. Throw a loaf of bread to each one and they will calm down and let you pass. Then hurry and take the Water of Life. You must leave with it before the clock strikes twelve or the gate will close and lock you inside."

The prince thanked him, took the iron rod and two loaves of bread, and went on his way.

Everything happened as the dwarf had said. The prince knocked three times with the iron rod and the castle gate flew open. In the courtyard lay two lions with their huge mouths open and their sharp teeth glistening. He threw each a loaf of bread and they quieted down.

The prince walked into the castle. He came to a big hall, where many enchanted princes sat around a long table. They did not move, nor did they speak. The king's youngest son took the rings from each one's fingers, and picked up a sword and a loaf of bread that lay near them on the floor.

In the next room, he found the most beautiful princess he had ever seen. He fell in love with her then and there.

The princess was so happy to see him that she kissed him joyously. "You have set me free," she said. "If you come back to me in a year we will marry and my kingdom will be yours."

Then she told him how to find the hidden courtyard where the Water of Life flowed. "But hurry. You must draw the water before the clock strikes twelve."

The prince promised to return in a year's time, and went on.

Along his way, he came into a room that held a freshly made bed. It looked so inviting, and he was so tired, that he lay down and fell asleep.

He awoke with a start as the clock was striking a quarter to twelve. He jumped from the bed in fright and ran into the courtyard of the castle.

There stood the fountain, and from it flowed the Water of Life. He quickly filled a cup with the precious liquid and, just as the clock was striking twelve, left through the castle gate. On the last stroke, the gate closed with such force that it took off a piece of his heel.

All the same he was happy to have the Water of Life, and he started homeward to his father.

After a while he met the dwarf again, and he stopped to thank him. When the dwarf saw the sword and the loaf of bread, he said, "The sword and loaf of bread will be great treasures to you. The sword can defeat entire armies, and the loaf of bread will never grow smaller no matter how much is taken from it."

The prince did not want to go home to his father without his brothers. "Good dwarf," he said, "do you know where my brothers are? They set out before me to find the Water of Life, but they have never returned."

The dwarf said, "They are stuck fast, wedged between two mountains. I cursed them, because they were so proud."

The prince begged the dwarf to release them, and at last the dwarf set them free. But he warned the prince, "Beware of your brothers. They have evil hearts."

Nonetheless the prince was glad to see his brothers again. They listened closely as he told them about finding the Water of Life and filling a cup with the liquid to take to their dying father. They bent their heads to hear when he described the beautiful princess and told them of her promise to marry him and make him prince of a great kingdom if he returned in a year's time.

Then the three of them rode away together on the long trip home.

They came to a land where war and famine raged. Destruction and starvation so afflicted the place that its king believed all was lost. The youngest son went to him and gave him the loaf of bread. With it the king fed his entire kingdom, and yet the loaf of bread remained whole. The prince then gave him the sword, and with that the king destroyed the invading armies and peace reigned over the land.

The prince took back the loaf and the sword, and the three brothers rode on. Twice more on their journey they came to lands that war and famine had brought nearly to ruin. Each time the prince lent the king the loaf of bread and the sword, and each time the people were fed and the kingdom was saved. But the loaf remained whole, and the sword did not stop shining.

In this way, the youngest prince saved three kingdoms and earned the eternal gratitude of three kings.

The brothers then boarded a ship and sailed across the sea. During the voyage, the two older brothers said to each other, "He has the Water of Life, and we have nothing. He will save our father's life and inherit the kingdom that should be ours by birth. And we will have nothing in the end as well."

They burned with anger and yearned for revenge. Together they plotted to destroy their youngest brother. While he slept, they emptied the Water of Life from his cup and poured it into one of their own. Then they filled his cup with bitter sea water.

As soon as they arrived home, the youngest son went to his father. He gave him the cup that he believed held the Water of Life, expecting him to drink from it and become well again. But instead, the king took a sip, spat the bitterness out of his mouth, and grew sicker than before.

As he lay in misery, the two older sons came in to him and accused their younger brother of trying to poison him.

"We have the Water of Life," they said, and gave their cup to the king. The moment he took one swallow, his sickness began to leave him. Before long he was as healthy and strong as he had been in the days of his youth.

When the two older brothers saw the youngest son, they laughed at him. "You found the Water of Life, but we took it away from you. You did all the work, but we will get all the reward. You should have kept your eyes open—we took it from you while you were asleep.

"Not only that," they said to him, "in a year one of us will go to the beautiful princess and claim her. One of us will be prince of her kingdom, not you.

"Furthermore," they said, "do not go to the king our father and tell him what we have done. He thinks you have betrayed him and he will not believe you.

"Besides that," they said, "if you say one word, we will kill you. If you want to live, you must keep silent."

The king, now restored to strength, was furious at his youngest son, who he thought had tried to murder him. So the king called his council together, and they sentenced the youngest prince to be shot in secret.

The prince suspected nothing. One day he went hunting, and the king's huntsman was ordered to go with him. When they were deep in the forest, the prince saw that the huntsman looked very sad.

"Good huntsman," he said, "what is the matter?"

"I must not tell you," the huntsman answered, "and yet I should."

"Say whatever it is. I swear I will forgive you," the prince said.

"Alas, my prince! I must kill you. The king your father has commanded it."

Filled with horror, the prince said, "Huntsman, do not kill me! Give me my life."

"Dear prince, I must kill you," the huntsman said sadly, and he raised his gun.

"Wait!" the prince said. "Stop! Give me your huntsman's clothes and take my royal garments in exchange, and I will escape into the forest."

"With gladness," the huntsman said. "I would never have been able to shoot you."

And so the huntsman went home by back roads where no one would see him in the prince's clothes, and the prince wandered deeper into the forest disguised in the simple clothes of the huntsman.

Some time after this, three wagons filled with gold and jewels came to the king for his youngest son. They were sent in gratitude from the three kings whose kingdoms the prince had saved with his sword and miraculous loaf of bread.

"Can my son have been innocent?" the king thought to himself. "Alas, I am sick at heart." Out loud he said, "How I wish he were alive! I will never forgive myself for having him killed."

At that the huntsman spoke up. "He is still alive. I could not bring myself to kill him." And he told the king what had happened.

A weight fell from the king's heart. He immediately sent a proclamation throughout his kingdom saying that his son should come home, where he would be welcomed with happiness and love.

In the meantime, the beautiful princess had her servants build a road, made of pure and shining gold, that led straight to the castle gate.

She said to her guards, "The man who rides straight to me up the center of the golden road is the right man, and you are to allow him to enter. But any man who rides to one side or the other of the golden road is not the right man, and you are not to let him in."

When the year was almost over, the oldest son decided it was time to go to the princess. He expected to pass himself off as her savior, and so claim her and her kingdom for his own.

When he saw the golden road gleaming in the sun, he said, "It would be a terrible shame to ride on a road as wonderful as this." He turned his horse to the side, and rode up to the castle along the right side of the golden path.

When he reached the castle, the guards said, "You are not the right man." And he was turned away at the gate.

Closer to the year's end, the second son went off to claim the princess and her kingdom. When he came to the golden road and his horse had set just one hoof upon it, he said, "It would be a thousand pities for a horse to tread on a road as beautiful as this." And he rode his horse along the left side of the road.

When he reached the castle, the guards said to him, "You are not the right man." And he too was turned away.

At exactly the year's end, the youngest son decided to leave the forest and his sorrows behind him and go to his princess. He rode along thinking only of her, wishing only to be with her. And so when he came to the road he did not notice it was made of gold. He rode quickly right up the center of its shining surface, straight to the princess's castle.

When the guards saw this, they said to him, "You are the right man." They opened the gates wide to allow him to enter.

The princess greeted him joyfully. "You are my savior, and the lord of my kingdom."

They were married with great celebration and much rejoicing throughout the land.

Then the princess told the prince that his father had forgiven him and wanted him to come back home.

With happiness in his heart, the prince returned to his father. He told the king how his brothers had tricked him and forced him to remain silent.

The king wanted to punish his two sons, but by that time they had sailed away over the sea. They never came back as long as they lived.